**Zeki and Daddy are going to swimming class tomorrow.**

**Daddy helps Zeki with his swim nappy and trunks.**

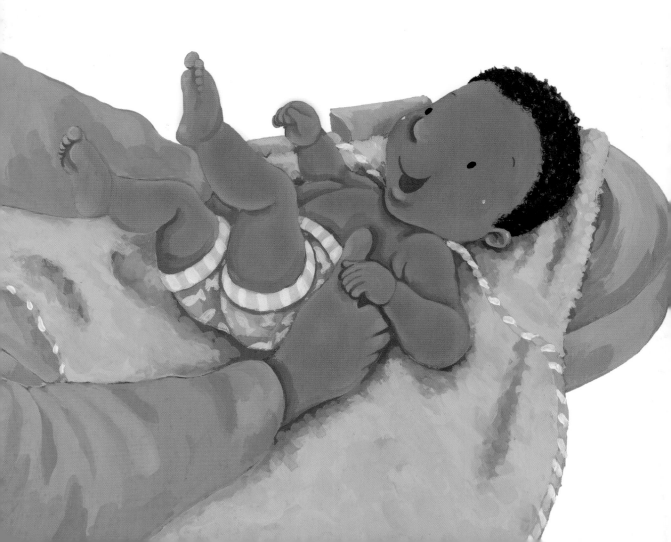

**Everything else goes into the locker.**

Everyone says hello.

# The babies sit on the edge of the pool.

**When the class is ready
the babies slide in.**

# First, they sing a splashy song.

Then, off they go!
Kick! Kick! Kick!

They swish and swooosh!

They splish and sploOOSh!

Then they pretend
Zeki is Baby Fish
and Daddy is
Daddy Fish.

Next it's off to the shower.
They use sloshy soap. . .

**and sloppy lotion.**

# Being a little fish is a lot of work!

After a quick snack,
Zeki is fast asleep.

To Milena, Mariell, and Iwona: baby fish, mummy fish, and granny fish!
—A. McQ.

To Immie, my little fish, from Mummy with love—R. H.

And with thanks for their advice, Siblings Afro Hair Design, Slough

Published in the UK & Ireland by Alanna Max
38 Oakfield Road, London N4 4NL
Zeki Can Swim! © 2021 Alanna Max
Text copyright © 2017 Anna McQuinn
Illustrations copyright © 2017 Ruth Hearson
Zeki Can Swim is part of the Zeki Books series developed by and published under licence from Anna McQuinn.
www.AnnaMcQuinn.com
www.AlannaMax.com
Printed in China
ISBN 978-1-907825-32-3